nickelodeon

Dora's Christmas Carol

Based on the screenplay "Dora's Christmas Carol Adventure"
by Chris Gifford

Illustrated by Dan Haskett and Brenda Goddard

A GOLDEN BOOK • NEW YORK

randomhouse.com/kids
Educators and librarians, for a variety of teaching tools, visit us at
randomhouse.com/teachers
ISBN: 978-0-307-97592-8
Printed in the United States of America
10 9 8 7 6 5 4 3 2 1

It was the night before Christmas. Dora was getting ready for her *Nochebuena* party. She and Boots had a lot to do.

Dora's *Nochebuena* party was the best of the year. Everyone put on their nicest clothes. There were all kinds of tasty treats. Benny really liked *los caramelos.*

Swiper was excited about the party, too—excited for his chance to swipe the star from the Christmas tree!

"Oh, no," Dora said. "If Swiper swipes on Christmas Eve, Santa will put him on the Naughty List—and he won't get any presents!"

Still, Swiper tried to swipe the Christmas star!

Just then, Santa flew out of the sky and landed at Dora's party. He had warned Swiper many times not to swipe.

"I'm afraid I'll have to put you on the Naughty List," Santa told Swiper.

"Santa, is there anything we can do to get Swiper off the Naughty List?" Dora asked. "I really want to help him."

Santa thought for a moment. "If Swiper can learn the true meaning of Christmas, I will change my mind," he said.

Santa gave Dora a card with a picture of a Christmas tree on it.

"Each time Swiper learns about the spirit of Christmas, a decoration will magically appear on the tree," Santa said. "He must get four ornaments and a star."

To learn about the meaning of Christmas, Dora and Swiper had to travel through time! First they needed to visit the past, when they were babies. Then they had to go to the future, when they would be big kids. Santa said the Grumpy Old Troll could help them with his magic!

And with that, Santa waved good-bye as his sleigh soared off into the sky.

Dora and Swiper quickly ran to the Grumpy Old Troll's bridge. The Grumpy Old Troll gave them magical time-travel capes.

"To make the capes work, you have to shake, shake, shake," the Troll explained.

Dora and Swiper put the capes on and started to shake them.

Magical sparkles swirled around Dora and Swiper, and they flew high into the air. When they landed, Dora and Swiper were still at the bridge, but the Grumpy Old Troll was now a Grumpy *Little* Troll! They had made it to the past!

As Dora and Swiper journeyed through the Christmas Forest, they met a puppy with a bone. Swiper wanted to swipe it. Then he remembered what Santa had said, and he didn't swipe the puppy's bone!

Suddenly, an ornament appeared on his card.

"I must be learning the meaning of Christmas," Swiper said. Then he and Dora continued farther into the forest.

"Look!" Dora exclaimed. "We know those babies! They're Isa, Boots, Tico, Benny, and Swiper when they were little!"

Just then, Baby Swiper sneaked out of his crib and swiped the other babies' Christmas toys. All the babies started to cry.

"Nobody should cry on Christmas," Swiper said, and he returned the Christmas toys to the babies. But as he did this, Baby Swiper swiped his cape.

"Baby Swiper, no swiping," said Swiper.

As Swiper took his cape back, another ornament appeared on his card.

"You have two ornaments now," Dora said. "Come on! Let's keep going so you can learn more about the Christmas spirit—and get off Santa's Naughty List."

Dora and Swiper shook their capes and traveled through time again.

When Dora and Swiper landed, they saw themselves. But they weren't babies anymore—they were little kids! And they were playing with their Christmas gifts.

"I remember when Santa gave me that rocking horse," Dora said.

"I loved that bunny," Swiper said.

The rest of Dora's friends were little kids, too. And they all really liked their Christmas gifts.

Even though Little Swiper had his own toy, he started swiping everyone else's Christmas gifts.

"This is terrible!" exclaimed Swiper. "I'm going to help them get their gifts back!"

Swiper searched everywhere. He looked under rocks and behind bushes. Soon Swiper had found all the missing toys Little Swiper had swiped and returned them to everyone.

"Look, Dora!" cried Swiper. "My card has three ornaments on it! Now I only need to find one more and the star."

"We need to go into the future, when we'll be big kids," said Dora. "Come on! Let's get you off the Naughty List. *¡Vámonos!*"

"Dora, are we in the future now?" asked Swiper as they landed after their magical journey.

"I think so," replied Dora. "Look! There I am, but as a big kid!"

Dora and Swiper introduced themselves to Big Kid Dora. Big Kid Dora was sad. Over the years, Swiper had swiped all the Christmas decorations. Now there were no more Christmas parties!

"But Swiper promised not to swipe on Christmas anymore," said Dora.

"Yes," said Swiper. "I'm learning the true meaning of Christmas."

"That's fantastic," said Big Kid Dora. "If you learn the true meaning of Christmas, maybe you'll stop swiping! And we can have our Christmas parties again!"

Just then, Older Swiper jumped out from behind a bush. He wanted to swipe Swiper's time-travel cape!

Everyone said, "Swiper, no swiping!" But Older Swiper wouldn't listen. Ever since he'd been put on Santa's Naughty List, no one could stop him from swiping. Older Swiper ran away with the cape.

Without the cape, Swiper couldn't travel through time.

"Now I'll never get off the Naughty List," he moaned.

"We have to get your cape back," Dora said. "And I know some amigos who can help."

They were Isa, Benny, Tico, and Boots! And they were all big kids!

"We'll help you learn the meaning of Christmas spirit," said Big Kid Boots.

Swiper was very happy that his friends were so kind.

"How will we find Older Swiper?" Boots asked.

"Let's ask the Maps," Dora said.

Map and Older Map said that to find Older Swiper, they had to follow the Wrapping Paper Trail to the Castle.

Dora and her friends quickly found the Wrapping Paper Trail. It was littered with torn wrapping paper.

"When Old Swiper opens his gifts, he just throws the paper on the ground!" said Boots.

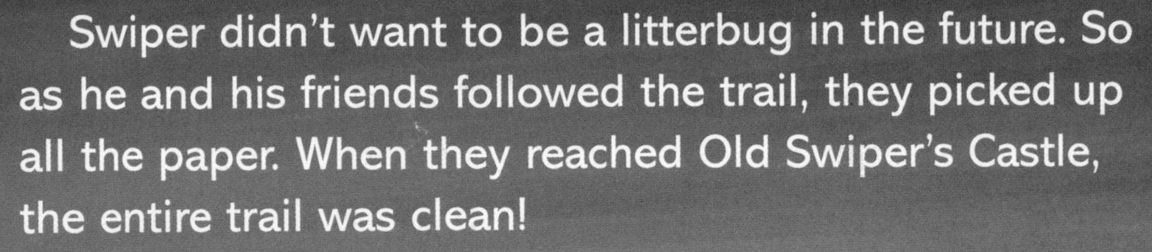

Swiper didn't want to be a litterbug in the future. So as he and his friends followed the trail, they picked up all the paper. When they reached Old Swiper's Castle, the entire trail was clean!

The friends entered the Castle and found Older Swiper. He was sleeping in a room filled with all the Christmas gifts he had ever swiped.

"I look so lonely," Swiper said. "I have lots of gifts, but I don't seem happy."

When the friends searched for the cape, they found all their missing Christmas gifts from over the years! Swiper even found the stuffed bunny he had loved when he was little.

Everyone was very happy when Swiper returned their gifts.

At last, Swiper found his cape and received the fourth ornament on his card. He knew he couldn't have done it without the help of his friends.

Before he left for home, Swiper looked at Older Swiper. He knew he didn't want to be lonely in the future like Older Swiper. Having friends was much better than swiping things.

So, with a shake of their capes, Dora and Swiper flew back in time.

Dora and Swiper returned to the *Nochebuena* party. Before the party started, Swiper gave Dora a gift. It was his stuffed bunny.

"This was my favorite toy as a child," Swiper said. "I want you to have it because you're such a good friend."

Dora gave Swiper a big hug.

Swiper finally understood that it is better to share than to take. "And you should always let your friends know you care," he said.

Suddenly, a gold star appeared at the top of the tree on Swiper's card. Bells began to jingle in the distance.

Santa had returned! He was very impressed by everything Swiper had learned.

"I'm taking you off the Naughty List!" Santa said.

It was a wonderful *Nochebuena* party—and a very merry Christmas.

"¡Feliz Navidad!"
everyone cheered.